Louis E Thayer

Jim and his Old Cornet

And Other Poems

Louis E Thayer

Jim and his Old Cornet
And Other Poems

ISBN/EAN: 9783337408923

Printed in Europe, USA, Canada, Australia, Japan

Cover: Foto ©Andreas Hilbeck / pixelio.de

More available books at **www.hansebooks.com**

JIM AND HIS OLD CORNET.

BY

LOUIS E. THAYER.

CINCINNATI, OHIO.
THE EDITOR PUBLISHING CO.
1898.

"The old, old Love Lane."—p. 23.

Table of Contents.

—

Contents.

Jim and his old cornet.

PROEM.

Think well of these—my songs—though they may be
But voiceless lines of syllables to thee.
Through them a secret hope, I would confess,
And if their dreary tones are meaningless,
Still listen as to troubled, moaning seas—
Or dream of winds that sob in forest trees.
        Think well of these.

Think well of these—my songs—for what they mean
To me. Each day the sunlight, thou hast seen
Unthinking—yet one ray lost from man's sin,
Through prison bars is worlds to him within.
These songs, to me, must either soothe or tease
But you, who read songs only at your ease—
        Think well of these.

And so I ask you—let the words suffice;
Not that the songs you hear be called for twice,
Not that you greet them with a loud applause,
Seeking to find their origin or cause.
But as you listen to the troubled seas,
Thus wed my secret to this passing breeze—
        Think well of these.

JIM AND HIS OLD CORNET.

Somehow Jim Foster never took
Like other boys to schoolin';
He'd never look into a book,
But allus keep a-foolin'.
The teacher used to say—says he,
"Jim Foster, you air goin' to be
A tarnal fool; jes' wait and see."
And Jim he used to wink at me,
And kind o' wrinkle up his phiz
Like when he played that air cornet of his.

Used to tease his dad, Jim did,
To stop his schoolin' and to let
Him waste his time, like, for a spell
Jes' playin' on his old cornet.
But the old man didn't jes' agree
To this and to Jim, one day says he,
"You be the boy you ought to be,
Or you will have a fuss with me."
Said if he didn't 'tend to biz
He'd smash that dern cornet of his.

Every time a circus cum to town
Jim never camed to school,
But allus used to hang aroun'
And with the band things fool.
Old man went one day, he did,
Said this time he would jes' get rid
Of Jim's cornet, and raised the lid

Jim.

Of his air trunk; but Jim had hid
All traces from what eyes might quizz
After that air cornet of his.

Well, time went on—we left the school:
I went into this store as clerk,
And Jim, our class's biggest fool,
Started off in search of work.
At first they gave me for my pay
Jes' thirty cents—no more—a day,
And all 'at I have got to say,
The work I did wan't light as play;
And in my mind each day there riz
Pictures of Jim and that air cornet of his.

For long didn't hear much 'bout Jim;
Cum right to fact didn't hear that.
Didn't know nothin' 'tall 'bout him,
But wondered every day what he was at.
Daily paper cum to me one day,
Looked to see what it had to say,
Strange it didn't cum in the usual way,
But through the mail without no pay.
I seen a picture, says I: "Sure 'tis
Jim and that air cornet of his."

Well this is the long and short of it,
Jim when he went away had met
A music man who heerd him play
A tune on that air old cornet.
And now Jim's leader of a band,
And though for a fool we thought him planned,
More 'an fifty men move at his command;
Ten dollars a day he gets to stand
And shake his fist or wave his hand,
And sometimes to carry to his phiz,
And play that air cornet of his.

AUTUMN'S MANTLE.

A mantle of green and gold
Lieth upon the lawn;
The shroud of a summer gone,
The shade of a charm withdrawn,
The dream of a faded dawn—
Life with its gloom and cold—
A mantle of green and gold.

A mantle of gold and green
Covers the garden walk;
A bud from a shattered stalk,
The sting of hopes that mock,
Dead lips that cannot talk,
The shadow of things unseen—
A mantle of gold and green.

A mantle of gold and green—
A mantle of green and gold.
Beauty and pride are rolled
Low in the damp and mould.
Where is the world's proud mien?
Look 'neath the green and gold—
Search 'neath the gold and green.

THINKIN' OF MY SWEETHEART.

I used to have a sweetheart, in the days gone by;
And someway I can't forget her—no matter how I try.
The roses but remind me of the velvet of her cheek,
And the bird's song seems to whisper jes' the way she used
  to speak.
And so I can't forget her and her kind and lovin' ways,
For my heart is weary, countin' all these dreary, lonely
  days,
That I wander on my pathway, keepin' back the tears and
  sighs,
And thinkin' of my sweetheart and the dream-look in her
  eyes.

There's something in the breezes like the rustle of her dress,
But she comes no more to greet me with her one-time sweet
  caress.
The perfume of the flowers seems not pure like that of yore,
And the stars seem twinklin' dimmer than they ever did
  before.
This life—it does not hold me in that old-time charm and
  bliss,
And I dream more of a future life, while thinkin' less of this.
For something holds me closer, so that hope within me
  cries,
"You will meet again your sweetheart with the dream-look
  in her eyes."

I used to have a sweetheart in the days of long ago,
But she left me for a vision that the blessed only know:

And now I've but a flower in a simple locket pressed—
And the humble place out yonder where they laid her at her
    rest.
But someway I can't forget her, for I'm seein' every day,
Signs and things in nature that remind me of her way.
The flowers and the grasses, the breezes and the skies,
Seem to speak of my old sweetheart and the dream-look in
    her eyes.

THE DREAM WEB.

The little lad wandered away last night—
  Away from the land of the sun;
And he swung to a land of purer light,
  In a web that the dream fairies spun.
"Goodnight," he said as he left us here,
  But he came not back with dawn;
The hours are long and the day is drear
  Since the little lad is gone.

Who can tell of the sights he saw
  As he swung in that soft dream web?
Doubtless he reached the river's side
  When the tide was at its ebb.
So perhaps he said, "The world's way back
  And this river is not so wide;
I can easily find this beaten track."
  So he crossed to the other side.

Ah', no one has left for a moment life
  And crossed to that other shore,
And returned again to this world of strife
  To cheer those they cheered of yore.
So the little lad who said "Goodnight"
  Comes not with his one time cheer,
For the dream web swung to the land of light,
  To never again swing here.

15

THE HOT DAYS COMIN'.

Oh! I am a-waitin' fer the hot days comin'—
    The hot days of summer when the temperature will rise,
When the sun'll be out shinin' an' the bees will be a-hummin'
    An' the old grey mare'll keep a-switchin' off the flies.
Them are the days that suit a feller loafin',
    When the grass is withered and the medder brook is dried:
When he can lie an' waller in the sunshine,
    With the freckles on his face an' the sunburn in his hide.

Oh! here in the country, when it's ninety in the shade,
    When the sweat is runnin' like a river down your face;
When all the world an' nature is sluggish! sluggish!!
        sluggish!!!
    An' when a lazy feller ain't a-feelin' out of place.
That's where I want to be—shiftless like an' home-like,
    Loafin' in my shirt sleeves with my boots thrown at my
        side;
With the butterflies around me an' the old sun shinin'
    An' everything jes' easy an' me satisfied.

When the medder flowers have been dried up by the sun,
    An' the road's dry an' dusty an' the suckers run up stream;
When the snake is out a-sunnin' an' the lily pads are
    covered
    With the frogs that sit in comfort an' in idle moments
    dream.
When the bumble-bee is lookin' fer something new with
    honey,
    An' the cat is a-sleepin' at the mouth of some rat hole—

"When he can lie and waller in the sunshine."

That's jes' the time fer a feller to be happy
  An' he will be if he happens to be havin' any soul.

Oh! I am a-waitin' fer the hot days a comin',
  When the hours are filled with sunshine an' there's sel-
      dom any rain;
When a feller feels like loafin' an everything around him,
  Ain't like it is in usual, but is twice as bright again.
Oh! I'm jes' waitin' fer the hot days comin'—
  The hot days of summer when the temperature will rise;
When the sun'll be out shinin' an' the bees will be a-hum-
      min',
  An' the old grey mare'll keep a-switchin' off the flies.

NOT NOW GOODBYE.

No need of a goodbye now;
The last leaf clings to the bough.
True, sun and stars and moon
Die all too soon—too soon!
But stifle this vain regret—
Is there need for a goodbye yet?

No need of a goodbye now;
Still clings dead joy on the brow—
Joy, since seared into grief,
Lone as the last fall leaf;
But still can'st thou forget?
Is there need for a goodbye yet?

Be still, heart, yet a while,
Watching the fading smile;
Wait till it all shall fade—
Parting is still delayed,
Life's closing breath shall sigh,
Some day, " goodbye ! "

THE THREE TOASTS.

" My toast is to love!" the young man cried,
  And he filled his cup to the brim;
A maiden fair sat at his side,
  And coquettishly smiled at him.
" Love that is ever fair and young,
  And the woman whom it is safe to wed—
The sweetest of all songs ever sung;
  Then here's to love," he said.

" My toast is to hate!" the young man cried,
  And he filled his cup to the brim;
And the maid at the table's further side,
  Flushed as she looked at him.
" Hate, that will not betray like love,
  Hate, with all affection dead;
I toast no more the sorrows of
  Love—let's drink to hate," he said.

" My toast is to love!" the young man cried,
  And he filled his cup to the brim;
" I will forgive her now," he sighed,
  And he drew the cup to him.
" I'll drink to love—'tis the better way,"
  He murmured, turning the beaker up,
And he quickly drank his life away
  As he drained the drug in the cup.

19

THE OLD SUN'S TRYIN' HARD TO SHINE.

It's been mighty nigh a blizzard and the snow's heaped
    high,
And the world has gone and give us a treacherous-lookin'
    sky;
The business men are huggin' their furnaces at home,
For the weather don't induce them toward their offices to
    roam.
And I am here a-loafin' when I orter be at work,
But times will come when every man his duties has to
    shirk.
The weather's mighty ugly, but I ain't a-goin' to pine,
For the old sun's tryin' its very best to shine.

Oh! the snow has gone and drifted as it hadn't orter do—
I'm afeared there'll be a circus when the teams go breakin'
    through;
And the man who braves the storm is in every sense a hero,
For ain't the old thermometer a dozen under zero?
Yes, it's driftin' and it's siftin' and the wind is jes' a
    blowin',
And it's freezin' and I'm sneezin', but it doesn't stop
    a-snowin'.
The sleet jes' hangs in bushels from the honeysuckle vine,
But the old sun's tryin' its very best to shine.

MY KIND.

My kind o' poet is the feller that has got
A cheerful voice for singin', if its accent is untaught:
The voice that pours its music all around you sweet an' free,
Jes' about like so much sunshine—say, that's the voice for
    me.
I like to read a poem a man can understand,
When the meanin' o' the poet ain't jes' dragged in under-
    hand:
Where the meter's kind o' slipp'ry an' the rhyme ain't hard
    to find—
An' the poet with such poetry is jes' about my kind.

My kind o' preacher is the preacher hates to dwell
Upon these thoughts o' pain an' tears, an' death, an' fire,
    an' hell.
That ruther talk o' heaven an' the good God waitin' there,
An' the good we should be doin' all around us everywhere.
The preacher that's as willin' to grasp the hardened hand
O' the workin' man as the millionaire—o' course you un-
    derstand:
The man that gives you comfort when with tears you're
    nearly blind,
If he never went to college—all the same he's jes' my kind.

My kind o' sweetheart is the one who ever tries
To do her best to please you, an' who tells you with her
    eyes
That she loves you—oh! far better than your rivals for her
    smile,

An' keeps her heart an' your heart tuned together all the
    while.
The girl that makes you better when her purity you see;
The girl that makes you happy—jes' as happy as can be;
The girl you're going to ask some day, her life with yours
    to bind.
She's the sweetest kind o' sweetheart an' is jes' about my
    kind.

THE OLD, OLD LOVE LANE.

There used to be a place, some distance from the highway,
A real enchanting by-way,
Now, that fairies only know: ·
    Where care was quite a stranger,
    And there wasn't any danger
In the old, old love lane where the roses used to grow.

There all was love and beauty, there all was joy and mirth;
'Twas the dearest spot on earth—
The old love lane of long ago;
    And in light the old moon decked her,
    While the flowers gave their nectar,
To the old, old love lane where the roses used to grow.

It was long years ago that my love there was plighted,
And my hopes were not blighted
In the old love lane of long ago;
    Then the moon shone bright above
    As my sweetheart told her love
In the old, old love lane where the roses used to grow.

We were wedded, and in joy we spent the coming years,
And never dreamt of tears,
While the joys so free did flow;
    And whene'er we spoke of love,
    Came a tender vision of
The old, old love lane where the roses used to grow. ‚

Years have passed away, and with them pleasures I have
    known—

I wander sad and lone
In the old love lane of long ago.
   There's a mound where dead leaves fall,
   And a rose bush—that is all
In the old, old love lane where the roses used to grow.

A DREAM.

Was it a dream and was it sleep's soft pinion
  That bore me far away from worldly thought,
To revel in a far and fair dominion
  Of beauty, fairy workmanship had wrought?
Ay! 'twas a dream—last night I fell a-sleeping,
  And earth to me was but a happy mart
Where joy might be obtained, but on awaking
  Dissatisfaction filled my very heart.

KEEP ON HOPING.

Ain't no need to worry or to moan or to complain,
Good Lord's got some reason for deferring of the rain;
    But 'twill get here by and by.
We can only keep a-hoping, and a-waiting and a-praying
For the rain to come at last, and jes' to keep a-saying,
"The water's mighty scanty but I ain't a-going to cry
A tear until the day comes when the well runs dry."

Perhaps the water measures only jes' an inch or two,
And tastes each time you drink it kinder muddy like to you—
    'Twill be deeper by and by.
So jes' keep on a-hoping for the rain 'at's going to come,
And fall and fall until it fills your well up plum;
But don't you let a tear-drop trickle from your eye,
'Twill be time enough for that when your well runs dry.

Don't you ever get complaining 'cause your stock of joys is
    low,
While you've got a single one left, jes' sip it kinder slow:
    There'll be more by and by.
Jes' sip it kinder slow-like, it won't improve by keeping;
While you've got a joy left don't go a-weeping.
Stock of joys tomorrow may be running high—
Don't you do no weeping till the stock runs dry.

THERE'S NO ONE LIKE MOTHER.

A man gets mighty tired of this humdrum life, you know,
When every one is busy and he's jostled to and fro;
There's plaguy little leeway in the money-making street,
And a feller's got to be awake or jes' get off his feet.
And folks—if once they see him down, they never stop to
   cry,
But looking at him with a smile and jeer they pass him by.
There's very little sympathy, and when I'm feeling blue,
There ain't no one to stroke my head like mother used to do.

Sometimes in school when things went wrong and I got
      feeling sad,
There wa'n't no soothing touch on earth like that which
      mother had.
If she had sinned in everything, that touch she'd give my
      brow,
Would be enough to earn a place in Heaven for her now.
Sometimes when I was jes' cast down and things looked
      black as ink,
I'd sit down in a corner by myself and think and think!
And after I had thought awhile and half my tears had
      shed—
Then mother'd come and smile on me and gently stroke my
      head.

And yet, 'tis business now and wealth that folks are
      thinking of;
There's not much music for the ear—and that old home-
      like love

Has vanished like the faces that I used to kiss of yore;
And mother, she has gone away—I see her smile no more.
I'm jes' a big grown boy, that's all, and childish I suppose,
But all I want is jes' to be my mother's boy, and close
My eyes, someday, and know I'll wake, when all my tears
       are shed,
And see my mother smile and feel her gently stroke my
       head.

PARTED.

When we parted, years ago,
Both agreed 'twas better so;
Though she knew my love, and I
Knew she loved me—yet a sigh
Was the only thing to tell
Of the love ineffable,
And we whispered—whispered low,
" Goodbye, love—'twere better so."

I've remembered all these years
Her pale face made sweet with tears;
And her look of tenderness,
And the words left me to guess.
I've remembered too the pain,
That I felt as once again
Both together whispered low,
" Goodbye, love—'twere better so."

Then I little knew—but now,
Standing on the old hill's brow,
While the thoughts of long years pass—
Standing, where amid the grass
I can see a new-made mound,
Though my eyes in tears are drowned,
Feel that parting years ago,
Was for me, far better so.

THE SILENT HOUSE.

Pap's dead and buried and the old house's silent—
  Silent, save the creakin' of the old oaken floor,
And we've got to eat alone this mornin' in the kitchen,
  And the table looks twice bigger than it ever did before.

It never seemed so lonesome as it does here this mornin'
  And before I never noticed the creakin' of the floor;
Jes' every little while I stop and keep a lookin'
  As if expectin' Pap would be comin' in the door.

The clock has ticked so loudly that it made my head ache, so
  I jes' got up and stopped it though that wasn't really why—
And I feel so sad and lonely, that I wish it wasn't wicked
  For me to wish that I could jes' sit down right here and die.

And time, it goes so slowly—why! I've done the chores—
        and they
  Allus use to take me till an hour after noon;
But time is somehow slower, today, for all the workin'
  Is done—and I have done it, and done it all so soon.

I'm goin' to bed and try to shut my eyes to everything,
  And jes' to keep from watchin', all the time, that outside
        door;
For Pap's dead and buried and the old house's silent!
  And I'm sad and lonesome like I never was before.

THE ROAD TO SUCCESS.

The path to fortune is not paved
  With gold and jewels all the way;
And we must grope through darkest night,
  If we would reach the brighter day.
Through thickets where the poison grows,
  And briars twine, we oft must press,
O'er quicksands we must make our way,
  If we at last would find success.

POETRY.

The world's full of poetry and its poetry's mighty sweet.
It's hoverin' around you and it's grovelin' at your feet.
Some people never see it and its beauty cannot find,
But the good God had some reason and created 'em stone -
    blind.
There's poetry in the grasses, there's poetry in the breeze,
There's poetry in the flowers and there's poetry in the trees.
There ain't a place uncovered that poetry hasn't pressed —
The world's so full of poetry that the birds don't find much
    room to nest.

The world's full of poetry and the poetry's full of love,
And the whole thing's sweeter than the cooin' of the dove;
The hours move as smoothly as the never failin' stream,
And life is jes' as happy—jes' as happy as a dream.
There's lots of folks that sleep all day and wander 'round
    all night,
A moanin' o'er the darkness, but they never see the light;
To them the world ain't poetry—there's no song from pole
    to pole,
There's discord in their heart-strings and no poetry in the
    soul.

I can see the poetry in the sunshine and the dew,
And I can hear the music if the sky ain't allus blue;
We've got to have some trouble to make our feelin's blend;
There's heaps of fun in kissin' but the kisses have to end.
There's poetry all around us in the day and in the night,

In the stars and in the sunbeams, in the darkness and the
    light;
You take a feller, allus hears life's discord—not its song,
And you're mighty sure to know, you are, that feller's
    heart is wrong.

A CHRISTMAS QUERY.

What does the Christmas bring us, my dear?
Does it come to you with the same sweet cheer
That it did in the years which have onward rolled,
Since we were lovers in the days of old?
The flush of your cheek is faded now,
And a look of care has kissed your brow.
Tell me, my darling—no one can hear—
What does the Christmas bring us, my dear?

She answers me not but her eyes are wet,
And they seem to ask, "Can you forget?"
And then I think of the trundle bed,
Of the snowy pillow and curly head;
And I step to the door and softly peep
At the little fellow fast asleep;
And then to my eyes there comes a tear—
What does the Christmas bring us, my dear?

She looks at me as she takes my hand;
She speaks no word but I understand
How her thoughts are out where the sleet and rain
Are beating down with a cold refrain—
Beating down on the village hill
And the little lad who sleeps there still;
She says as she smiles through the sigh and the tear,
"It makes us the same old lovers, dear."

LIFE CHANGES SO.

Life changes so, 'tis hard to feel our way,
To labor on with faith from day to day;
To crush the cruel thorns beneath our feet,
To find the bitterness of what was sweet;
'Tis hard to trust, to feel and know—
      Life changes so.

Life changes so, with darkness, night and dawn;
The graves of love and joy forever yawn
In fields of flowers, finding for their dew
The tears of those whose loves were true;
When comes the rain, the heartache or the snow—
      Life changes so.

Life, Death and all these things are wed together;
So let the storm foretell the sunny weather;
Some years are moments and some moments years—
Smiles are but foretastes of the coming tears;
Life is uncertain, whither shall we go
      Life changes so.

IF I WAS MORE LIKE YOU.

Old friend, your hand you reach to me
To raise me, and with fervency
You strive to guide me on my way,
While words of happiness you say
To cheer me—you are kind and true—
I would that I were more like you.

" It is no trouble," so you say,
To help me o'er my rougher way.
You are so willing, good and kind,
That I—to selfishness inclined—
Stand here abashed before your view:
Oh, would that I were more like you!

Old friend, your virtue when I see
With eyes that can view worthily;
When I can feel your hand touch mine,
And know my touch is as divine—
When words I never misconstrue,
Then shall I be more like to you.

"So you sit there by the embers and the old brown Bible hold."

WHEN THE YEAR GROWS OLD.

There's a sort of tearful sobbing in the whisper of the rain,
And a half heart-broken throbbing as it patters on the pane.
The katydids are silent and the air is damp and cold—
Say, it's mighty sad and lonesome when the year grows old.

There's something in the darkness, keeps a heart from being
      light,
As it settles o'er the landscape when it isn't time for night.
There's a sort of haunting fancy 'bout the story you jes'
      told—
Say, it's mighty sad and lonesome when the year grows old.

There seems to be a dullness to your joking all the while,
And somehow it kind o' hurts you when there ain't no one
      to smile;
So you sit there by the embers and the old brown Bible
      hold—
Say, it's mighty sad and lonesome when the year grows old.

Somehow you get to thinking of the faces that ain't there:
The picture on the mantle and the long since empty chair.
And the tears will come to tease you as you sit there in the
      cold—
Say, it's mighty sad and lonesome when the year grows old.

THE LIGHT IN THE DARKNESS.

'Twas a wild, wild night. The angry sea
　Had lashed itself into silver foam,
And many a wife, on bended knee,
　Prayed in her little sailor home
For the husband out o'er the cruel deep,
　With the lightning flashing over him,
And the hungry waves that could not sleep
　In their eagerness to cover him.
Many a prayer went up that night
　From those little homes to the home above;
Lips that trembled with pain and fright,
　Uttered words of deepest love.

Never before had the waves so high
　Dashed in the harbor of Marcha:
Nor the lightning in the gloomy sky
　Pushed the clouds with such force away.
And the waves, on the rocks along the shore,
　Would break and utter an angry roar.
'Twas the wildest night—old sailors say,
　That ever fell on coast Marcha.

In a little cottage, there that night
　A maiden sat and wept alone,
Her heart was sad as her face was white,
　And she offered up a plaintive moan.
A childish face was her's and yet
　It bore the marks of womanhood:
Her lips were sadly, firmly set—

Her eyes spoke of the true and good.
She was a child, respecting years—
    A woman in experience;
A child that wept not childish tears—
    A child with woman's love and sense.

" 'Twas such a night as this," sighed she,
    " My brother's ship ran on the rocks,
'Twas such a night with such a sea
    As even now out yonder mocks:
And he was lost—oh, cruel sea,
    Dost thou still foam and laugh at me,
Not satisfied to clasp thy prey
    Must torture me in every way ? "

And then she started as she gazed
    Out through the window, and with eyes
By the mist of horror glazed,
    In a trembling voice she cries:
" The beacon father has not lighted !"
    Then she started and affrighted
Cried: " My Savior, guide and help me,
    Give me strength that I may brave be,
For my father has been captured
    By the wreckers of the sea !
They have seized him, and the beacon
    Does not shine off o'er the waves;
God protect the helpless sailors
    From the million yawning graves !
If the beacon is not lighted,
    Then the land sharks will be fed
With the plunder of dead sailors.
    I must light that light," she said.
" It is wild—the winds are angry;
    I must climb that fearful height,

Where the beacon should be burning—
   And it yet shall burn tonight."

She started on her journey,
   Tho' the winds blew fierce and wild.
And she murmured slowly, softly—
   " I'm a woman not a child."
Lightning flashed and crashed about her,
   Did she waver from her track ?
No, she toiled on mid the tempest,
   Thinking not of turning back.
Through the darkness came the signals
   Of a ship in sore distress,
And the thought that she might save it
   Strengthened more her faithfulness.
Still she hastened on excited,
   With a face all ghastly white
While her trembling lips repeated—
   " It shall shine, and bright tonight."

She reaches now the beacon ;
   She is faint and in a daze,
But she sets the light a-burning—
   'Tis a life-assuring blaze,
The ship sends back a signal—
   She has saved it from the deep,
But the waves about the harbor
   In a wilder frenzy leap.

Now beside the blazing beacon,
   Cold and still the maiden lies,
Her poor lips have done with whispers,
   Life has faded from her eyes.
By her side two men are kneeling;
   One a young man tall and strong,

But the other grey and aged—
  See! they kneel in silence long.
Then the young man speaks: "My father,
  I was near to death tonight,
I should now be cold and speechless,
  If she had not lit the light."
But the old man only murmured,
  "Oh, my brave girl I shall miss,"
And upon her marble forehead
  He pressed one simple kiss.

Sailors even now will tell you,
  Of that sad and dreary night—
Of the girl who saved her brother,
  How she lit the beacon light.
And so deep was the impression
  Of the deed—the sailors say,
That the wreckers ceased their wrecking
  On the rocky coast Marcha.

OUR LOVE.

Sing you a love song? I can sing
Of the snows of winter, the buds of spring;
The hopes that are faded, the friends that are gone,
The sorrow of night and the pleasure of dawn.
But the song of my heart, my lips cannot sing,
For 'tis sweeter than ever the bird song at spring—
Sweet as the dream of the future to be,
Is my love for you, dear, and your love for me.

The rose lives a season and withers away.
The butterfly lives the poor life of a day.
The grasses have withered, the robin has flown
And the beauty of nature has buried its own.
In the midst of this fading, our hearts must grow old;
And our eyes, dim with tears, see the world grim and cold:
But our hearts will keep warm as we constantly see
My love for you, dear, and your love for me.

Our hair will be silver, our lives nearly done;
But the pain of our hearts with the joy shall be one.
For through all the darkness, the pain and distress
Neither shall want for a tender caress.
And together we'll walk where the still waters flow—
Where there is no sorrow—where pure blossoms grow;
But none of them purer or fairer shall be
Than my love for you, dear, and your love for me.

THE DEAD PLAYMATE.

Wake up, Hallie, little Hallie! Don't you know that it is
    day.
Wake up! wake up! and come with me and we will romp
    and play.
Can't you see the sun shine or hear the robin's song?
Wake up, little Hallie! What makes you sleep so long?

What makes you lie so still and never answer when I call,
Don't you feel like romping 'round and playing with your
    ball?
And mamma, on your cheek big tears are trickling along—
Say, mamma, won't you tell me why Hallie sleeps so long?

Oh I am tired waiting for you to wake and play
With me—Say, Hallie, don't you know that it is day?
If you make believe you're sleeping when you ain't, it's
    awful wrong;
Please, mamma, won't you tell me why Hallie sleeps so long?

Oh I'm just a-feeling lonesome 'cause you always keep a-
    sleeping
When I call—while mamma sits there by your side and just
    a-weeping.
Oh can't you see the sun shine or hear the robin's song?
Say, mamma, won't you tell me why Hallie sleeps so long?

IN BOHEMIA.

In Bohemia,
Where the dark wine flows;
In Bohemia,
Where the wild night goes
With flashes of poetry, glints of song,
Where the long night does not seem so long;
Ho Captain! how far is the sail o'er the sea
To the land that seems beckoning ever to me,
To that land where the life is reckless and free?
Away to the land Fame's breezes have fanned,
Bohemia land! Bohemia land!

In Bohemia,
Oh to meet men of letters
In Bohemia,
Where Fame binds its fetters
About the heart, and places a pen
With a gentle hand in the hands of men.
Ho Captain! where lies the land I seek,
Where the Arts are bred and the Muses speak?
There the rich aid the poor, the strong the weak;
Away to that land where the magic wand
Touches Ambition—Bohemia land!

WHEN THE OLD YEAR DIES.

Take a feller fond of nature, an' it sets him feelin' blue,
When the bees have stopped their hummin' with their sum-
    mer's labor through;
When he wanders through the garden, where the flowers
    used to grow—
Where the grass is hidden from him by a coverlet of snow.
Say! you bet it makes him mournful, when he looks an' sees
    these things,
With the air all filled around him with imaginary wings.
It makes him feel discouraged, an' the tears come to his eyes,
But it finds him half heartbroken,
                When
                    the
                        old
                            year
                                dies.

When the bluebird leaves the woodland an' the robin leaves
    the brush,
An' the katydid's soft greetin' fades into a death-like hush;
When the dead leaves flutter downward an' the sky grows
    cold above—
Say! those hours are as bitter as a disappointed love.
You can hear the chill winds whisper, in a tone that's ever
    drear,
" There's a time for sobs an' sorrows, an' that time will soon
    be here."

Take a feller fond of nature, an' it draws his tears an' sighs:
You will find him sad an' pensive,
                  When
                      the
                         old
                            year
                                dies.

An' it makes but little difference, what the old year's days
      have seen.
You may hold a faded blossom or a bunch of evergreen.
The evergreen you cherish, an' you clutch the blossom tight,
But the world may hold the latter as the treasure that's
      most bright.
Somebody else's Christmas was a long, dark day for you—
Your holiday's a sad one an' sad not to a few,
But we mortals are all mourners that Death's angel, now,
      defies:
For he finds us half heartbroken
                  When
                      the
                        old
                         year
                            dies.

THE GOLDEN-ROD.

The tall haughty plumes of the golden-rod
Over the fence by the wayside nod.
They tell of the summer well-nigh gone,
And the autumn days that are coming on,
And the breezes whisper—whisper low,
Like the haunting voices of long ago—
" Cometh the autumn chill and cold
And already the year is growing old."

Where the golden-rod in its beauty grows,
We must seek in vain for one wild rose;
It blooms no more where it once was known
For the golden-rod reigneth there alone.
The birds prepare for a warmer clime,
And chant a song of solemn time—
" Cometh the autumn chill and cold
And already the year is growing old."

Though the golden-rod reigns and reigns supreme,
'Tis but the life of a pleasant dream.
It too, like the pink and rose, must fade
And its blossoms together with theirs be laid.
The snows will fall and the winds will blow,
And the only tale their songs will know—
" Cometh the winter chill and cold
And the life of the year is nearly told."

THAT NIGHT ON GILLING'S PLAIN.

That night we camped on Gilling's plain—
    We'd flung the weapons down.
A conquered band were we again,
    And the flask was passed aroun'.
We drank like men that might have been
    The victors—but instead,
A trampled band in a hostile land,
    With half our numbers dead.

Who thought of sleep? Not we who'd fought
    That ill-cursed day for life:
The mind had only room for thought
    Of children, friends and wife.
We—yes, brave men we may have been,
    And yet our heart-felt pain
Drove from us sleep and made us weep
    That night on Gilling's plain.

Before my eyes that whole long night,
    A ghastly form there stood;
A man, whose face was deathly white,
    While his hand was steeped in blood.
And I chilled with fright and hid the sight
    Of the figure from my eyes;
Tho' my eyes were blind, yet before my mind,
    That figure still would rise.

I saw again our leader meet
    The foe's untiring thrust,

And then beneath the horses' feet,
  Low trampled in the dust.
I saw it all—the colors fall,
  And half our numbers dead:
A scattered band we could not stand
  But mad with fright we fled.

It all came back that night to me,
  And filled my soul with dread.
What ill would come with dawn to me?
  Should I be one more dead?
And does God fight to aid the right—
  Are all my prayers in vain?
Thus every thought with pain was fraught,
  That night on Gilling's plain.

The day it dawned. My God! the sight
  Might well have veiled the sun.
Such pain were better hid in night—
  How had the field been won?
Loss of life had fed the strife!
  Then came the loud command
That we must fight for life e'er night—
  We fight—a drooping band.

At noon the foe appeared—a band
  Of forty thousand strong.
We scarcely had eight thousand,
  But were burning with our wrong.
Then came the fight; the steel flashed bright.
  For life we fought again—
Like madmen fought and none forgot,
  That night on Gilling's plain.

THAT NIGHT ON GILLING'S PLAIN.

Then came the cry of the retreat,
  And forward plunged the foe;
And tried to flee from the defeat
  Down to the plain below.
The fight was done, and all was won—
  We had not fought in vain:
For blood had bought the blood that stained
  The soil of Gilling's plain.

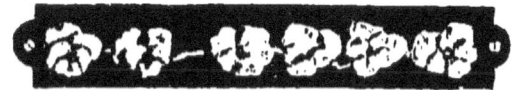

EARTH'S PARADISE.

All the world's a paradise of blossoms;
　All the world's a garden in full bloom,
Looking at the bright side and the right side—
　Looking at the sunshine—not the gloom.
Oh, to the heart that sees the blessings,
　Every month is just as sweet as June,
And April is a good time for rejoicing,
　To the heart that always keeps itself in tune.

Don't mourn because your place in life is humble.
　Upon the bush, there's no rose poor as this:
Tho' fairer ones may bloom when it is faded,
　It still will be the one some heart will miss.
The crowd may jeer at some poor, tired singer,
　And yet his song reach one weak, hungry heart,
The light may be a poor one—yet its beaming
　Cause some one on a better path to start.

Yes, all the world's a paradise of blossoms,
　In the meadow and the pasture and the wood;
And the breezes seem to say to man "Be noble!"
　While the birds all seem to sing to him "Be good!"
We move about in workings to the music
　Of the birds, the brooks, the breezes—and we hear
A kind of God-like strain throughout the music,
　That seems to lift us up on wings of cheer.

WHISPERING FANCIES.

Whispering fancies, lull me to rest,
  Safe on the breast of the days long gone by;
Sing me the songs that you can sing best—
  Sing me a soothing and sweet lullaby.

As a child may I pass to the city of dreams,
  To revel awhile in that realm where the gold
With a wonderful splendor and majesty gleams—
  In that realm where the people never grow old.

Whispering fancies, sing of the friends
  Who have passed over to wait me beyond:
Lead me to dream of a mother who bends
  And kisses my brow with a manner so fond.

Sing of dead love and hopes of my life—
  The loves and the hopes that lie buried away;
I am tired, tonight, of the world and its strife,
  So sing me a song of some long bygone day.

Oh, for a moment to rise and depart
  From this cold fickle world where treachery gleams
On each side; and to feel that rest in the heart
  That only is known in the city of dreams.

Whispering fancies, lull me to rest,
  Safe on the breast of days long gone by.
Sing me the songs that you can sing best—
  Sing me a soothing and sweet lullaby.

A SONG FOR THE PRESENT.

The years of long ago, oh ho!
The years of long ago;
They had their cold and they had their snow,
And the rains came down and the winds did blow,
And they had their days that were dark and drear—
So why not sing of the days now here?
Not the years of long ago, oh ho!
    Not the years of long ago.

The years of long ago, oh ho!
The years of long ago;
They had their days when hope burned low,
And we saw no star we were weepin' so,
Nor thought that a clearin' time was near.
So why not sing of the days now here?
Not the years of long ago, oh ho!
    Not the years of long ago.

The years of long ago, oh ho!
The years of long ago;
The roses are thick in this year's track,
And we haven't time to be lookin' back.
The air is sweet and the sky is clear,
So why not sing of the days now here?
Not the days of long ago, oh ho!
    Not the days of long ago.

WHEN THE BIRDS GIT BACK.

When I gaze out on the snow drifts and the cold grey win-
    ter sky,
I always think o' spring time, with the least bit o' a sigh.
O' course I'm warm and cozy, seated here the hearth before,
But the snow birds chirp and shiver jes' outside the cottage
    door.
Oh, I tell you what, it's dreary and the hours they are long
With no flowers in the garden and no birds to sing a song.
The woods are cold and silent and attractiveness they lack—
The world can't have its music till the birds git back.

I've strolled down by the pasture through the old bars and
    the pines,
And scraped the snow off lookin' for some checkerberry vines;
I wanted jes' to see them and I hunted kneelin' down
But the red had left the berries and the leaves were dull
    and brown.
It's lonesome in the pasture and the woods are sadly drear,
For the blue jay's mournful shriekin' is the only cry you hear.
The snow has wholly hidden the old worn wagon track
And the woods can't have no music till the birds git back.

I didn't see no bluebirds in the birches by the brook,
And hurriedly I passed them with a half regretful look:
I tried to dream 'twas springtime with the buddin' trees,
    you know,
But the snow lay all around me and I couldn't make it go.

Not thinkin' where I loitered, I wandered on and came
Down to the yellow birch tree where last spring I carved
      my name;
It nearly set me weepin' when I saw it there turned black—
And the heart can't have its music till the birds git back.

I made a total failure when I up and tried to sing—
There ain't no inspiration when gloom speaks in everything.
So I fell back onto thinkin' and my thoughts were sober too,
And I reached my home a-feelin'—well, a-feelin' rather blue.
I say it's cold and dreary on a real stiff winter day
And if you've got a home then that home's the place to stay;
For the woods are cold and silent and attractiveness they
      lack—
So the world can't have its music till the birds git back.

UNSELFISH LOVE.

If all the roses in the world
  Were your roses, dear,
And but one little faded bud
  Was mine to give me cheer,
I still would be more happy
  With that poor bud alone,
Than if the roses which you loved,
  Were all to be my own.

If all the joys in the whole world
  Were given you, my dear,
And Nature gave a smile to you,
  But brought to me a tear,
Ah! I would be far happier
  With that poor tear alone,
Than if the joys which now are yours
  Were all to be my own.

Yes, my dear, I love you so
  That were the joys all mine,
While 'round your life the pains and fears
  Would slowly, surely twine,
The quiet and the peace would fail
  To bring me joy or rest—
The rose I wore would deeply set
  Its sharp thorns in my breast.

"It's jes' my way."

IT'S JES' MY WAY.

Uncle Bill he used to say,
"Don't you mind, it's jes' my way,"
After he had said something
That had set me whimpering.
And he'd stroke my curly head—
"Don't you care 'bout what I said!
I'm a feelin' cross today!
Don't you mind, it's jes' my way."

"I'm a cross old fogy sure
If your noise I can't endure;
For the best boy you have been,
I ever saw for discipline."
Uncle Bill would talk like that—
And my curly head would pat.
"Dry your tears," he used to say,
"Don't you mind, it's jes' my way."

In the midst of business sway
Stands that boy, a man today,
Who in human nature sees
Men of many marked degrees.
And sometimes he thinks how few
To the world are clearly true—
True enough when cross to say,
"Don't you mind, it's jes' my way."

THE OLD FOREST PATH.

The old forest path! A memory of years
That have never been drowned in the sighs and the tears,
Which have marked the long days of a long dreary past,
Since the mystical day when I walked o'er it last.

Old Time for all of his marks of decay,
Touches some things with the brightness of day;
Eyes dim, but the scenes we often think of,
Are marked by the evergreen blossoms of love.

So the old forest path with the ivies that crept
Toward the brush where the night bird so restlessly slept,
That wound in and out as it flowed like a stream,
Still leads me away in a midsummer dream.

With songsters that sang, the partridge that whirred,
The squirrel that played, and the breezes that stirred
The leaves of the trees, as I wandered along,
With thoughts void of care and a heart full of song.

The old forest path! Does it still trace its way
Where the wild orchids grow and the red squirrels play?
I wonder—and sometimes a tear of regret
Clouds over the scene I can never forget.

I shall see it no more for 'tis far, far away,
As one of the charms which we pass in the day;
We pass by the rapture of perfume and light
But it after returns as a vision of night.

THESE DECORATION DAYS.

These Decoration Days are sad and lonely days for me,
The sun may shine and yet the skies seem dark as they
    can be;
For when we meet upon the Green, dressed in our army blue
I weep to think we're standing there so feeble and so few.

We mustered on the village Green one day I'll not forget,
My heart beat eager for the strife—I feel that throbbing yet;
Loved ones had gathered there their last words of goodbye
    to say,
And 'mid their tears and sobs and sighs, we turned and
    marched away.

And when we meet upon the Green—a mere handful of men;
And when I think of how we look and how we did look then,
It seems as though I couldn't stand awaiting the command
To march, besides my sobbing seems to more than drown
    the band.

And in the cemetery, where the flags fly in the breeze,
And where the banners are displayed up in the tops of trees,
'Twas there last year I stood and watched the folks as they
    went by
And then I hid behind them all lest they should see me cry.

And when the girls with buds and flowers, were going
    around the graves,
A-placing them with careless hand above the sleeping braves,

'Twas all that I could do to keep from taking off my hat
And claiming that the Veterans with their own hands
    should do that.

And then I wept and stood and thought, then brushed the
    tears away,
And looking up toward Heaven then—yes, then I tried to
    pray:
The prayer was kind of broken and my eyesight sort of
    blurred,
But the good God must have read my heart; if so my prayer
    was heard.

And when I turned to go I stooped and from a grave near by,
I plucked a flower, kissed it twice and yet I don't know why!
And then I turned and groped my way—for tears had filled
    my eyes,
And quietly I sought my home with sorrow and with sighs.

These Decoration Days are sad and lonely days for me,
The sun may shine and yet the skies seem dark as they
    can be;
For when we meet upon the Green, dressed in our army blue,
I weep to think we're standing there so feeble and so few.

FAME.

Time's hand may pour into Fame's golden cup,
   Year after year the magic liquid, yet
How soon the thirsty one has turned the beaker up,
   And drained it dry without his lips becoming wet.
Ah! how much fame could satisfy the soul?
   How much would cool the heart's desire?
How much success must Time's hand pour upon
   Ambition, if 'twould quench its raging fire?

SO HARD TO WAIT.

So hard to wait—the shadows are so long
In fading, and we hear no song
To cheer us in the darkness and the gloom.
Were there some sunshine or one bud in bloom,
'Twere easier to linger: but 'tis late,
The shadows are so long in fading—oh, so long—
      'Tis hard to wait.

So hard to wait—the darkness is so deep,
The troubled heart can find no rest nor sleep.
The wearied spirit bows itself in prayer,
And asks for strength to conquer its despair:
Oh! but 'tis bitter thus to feel cold fate,
The darkness is so deep—alas, so deep,
      'Tis hard to wait.

So hard to wait—the world seems so unkind;
The dawning light on these poor, tired, blind
And weeping eyes, will fall, we know, some day—
Some day! but that seems, oh so far away.
Teach us to love—we need not learn to hate,
The world seems so unkind—ah, so unkind
      'Tis hard to wait.

MY CASTLES.

I never have reared my castles
  As the poets do in Spain,
Nor dreampt of the frowning turrets,
  Looking far o'er the Spanish main.
For 'tis not in a future vision
  They build themselves—ah, no!
I have only the ivied ruins
  Of my castles of long ago.

I once built as costly castles
  As ever the bards sang of,
And peopled them with loved ones—
  Oh! what a dream of love.
The corridors rang with laughter
  Of children at their play;
But now the voices haunt me,
  As voices of yesterday.

The castles have crumbled and fallen.
  'Twas only a dream of light,
While darkness as black as the shade of death
  Floods through my heart tonight.
Take down the pictures that grieve me—
  Hide the one of the fair young wife,
And the other one with the merry face,
  And the eyes so full of life.

MY CASTLES.

Take down the one of the baby!
  Lay it tenderly away—
I've been dreaming—idly dreaming,
  Of my castles all the day;
Not Spanish castles founded
  In the days to come—ah, no;
Dreaming of ivied ruins—
  My castles of long ago.

ALL IS VANITY.

What has the king to boast over the slave?
    Naught but a throne.
An army shall fight and an army shall save
The ruler that reigns and the colors which wave:
But the king must give up his crown for the grave—
    Can he call it his own?

What have the rich to boast over the poor?
    Nothing but gold.
Riches that buy the things that allure,
They hold in a grasp which they dream is secure;
But gold purchases never the things that endure—
    But valueless things that are sold.

What have the strong to boast over the weak?
    Nothing but power.
Power to labor, and conquer and seek;
Strength to crush down the strength of the meek:
Yet what is this power when Death comes to speak—
    This strength of an hour?

The king is a man and the slave is a man,
    And both are but men for a day.
The deeds we can't do and the deed which we can,
    Will only too soon pass away.
The scepter shall fall from the hand that grows cold,
    And the king who forced armies to strife
Shall only be pitied with tears manifold,
    By the slave, who stands honored with life.

BON-FIRE SEASON.

I still can remember what feverish joy
  Was mine, when the smoke in the air
Told only too well to the heart of a boy,
  That a brush heap was burning somewhere.
My life has been filled with joys fair and bright,
  But I doubt if among them I've found
A joy that has brought me the perfect delight
  That with bon-fire season came 'round.

Oh! the heart of a boy is a land fair but strange,
  And one that great men have ignored;
For they have forgotten the limits and range
  Of the country they one time explored.
And so 'tis with me, it is hard to believe,
  As I think of my hopes still uncrowned,
That the heart now is weak, that naught could deceive
  When bon-fire season came 'round.

Does manhood but come to teach us how much
  We have lost in the boyhood gone by:
To taunt us of joys when have perished all such,
  And the dead leaves surrounding us lie?
I know not—but life never wakens my heart
  As it did in the days that are drowned,
In the tears I have shed—for that boy-loving art,
  Since bon-fire season came 'round.

SELF-MADE SORROW.

It is easy now to forget it—
   The unkind thing you say,
And perhaps you do not regret it—
   Oh, but you will some day.
Some day when the words come to you,
   And your pleasure and peace attack,
And with all of their sting pass through you,
   You will wish you could take them back.

It troubles you not while you do it—
   The wrong you do in play,
And perhaps you do not now rue it—
   Oh, but you will some day.
Some day, when the land you live in
   Is dark at the very dawn;
Made dark by the pain you give in
   The days that are dead and gone.

Some day will come and awake you
   With the same harsh words you said,
And memory arising shall make you
   A self-hewn passage tread.
The world will be full of faces,
   Pleading through long, dark years,
While your heart weary paces,
   A valley of self-made tears.

THE BUTTERFLY DAYS.

Oh, the butterfly days! the butterfly days!
   The hopes and the fears which they teach
As they lead us a chase through dark gloomy ways,
   And hover just out of our reach.
Ah, we see them sometimes as they pause o'er a flower,
   Or raise their bright wings in the sun:
But the darkness of night, a cloud or a shower,
   Drives them hence when the day is scarce done.

They rise o'er a hedge and we still follow on,
   They lead us through fields of bright flowers;
We follow all day and again with the dawn,
   Not heeding the fast flying hours.
Yes, man rushes out from his every-day cares
   And in the dark woodland he gropes,
While he breathes in a whisper his longings and prayers,
   For the butterfly days of his hopes.

Oh, the butterfly days! the butterfly days!
   We push and we crowd on our way,
And ever can see through the sunshine or haze,
   A place where our lives could be gay.
Poor fools! we know not that the dreams which we chase,
   Are only vain, hand-painted things;
A bright spot or two, we have seen fit to place,
   On a pair of dark dust-laden wings!

YOUR MA WANTS YOU.

There ain't much chance for a little chap to play,
Somebody allus has to holler out and say,
" Hey! Your Ma wants you."
Seems to think a little chap don't need no fun,
Nor time to frolic—" Hey! You'd better run,
      Your Ma wants you."

Had a circus wonst an' asked my best girl down
To see me in the ring, a showin' off as clown.
" Hey! Your Ma wants you."
Say, I was cuttin' ice, an' the show had jes' begun,
When the hired man yelled out, " Hey! You'd better run,
      Your Ma wants you."

Had a heated game of base ball yesterday.
I jes' had come to bat when some one had to say,
" Hey! Your Ma wants you."
" Paste her out, fetch in a score, we stand in need of one,"
The fellers yelled, an' then I heard, "Hey! You'd better run,
      Your Ma wants you."

There ain't much chance for a little chap to play,
Somebody allus has to holler out an' say,
" Hey! Your Ma wants you."
The world's chock full of work that ain't no fun—
Lie down to rest an'—" Hey! You'd best get up an' run,
      You Ma wants you."

DREAMING.

I wonder, tonight, as I sit here
  And gaze through the wearisome years,
That my heart grows so heavy and lonely,
  That my eyesight is clouded with tears;
There's a face which comes up in my memory—
  A face sweet and touching—but nay!
Why should I spend time for dreaming
  Of one whom the years took away?

I wonder, that vision comes to me,
  With such a sad touch of regret;
I wonder, that years have gone by me,
  But never have let me forget.
Such a sweet little thing—but she left me,
  That dark, dreary morning in May—
But why should I fall to dreaming
  Of one whom the years took away?

Ah! well, we dream of the roses,
  And the petals that withered and fell;
And we whisper, too late, the secrets
  Which our hearts have dreaded to tell.
And we dream of the birds and the sunshine,
  When the dark night has robbed us of day.
And thus too, it is I fall dreaming
  Of one whom the years took away.

70

"I in these flowery meads would be."

"I in these flowery meads would be."

AN APRIL REVERIE.

"I in these flowery meads would be;
These crystal streams should solace me."
—*Izaak Walton.*

The brook winds slowly on its way
  And sings a low, soft lullaby;
Its ripples laugh as if in play,
  And one by one they laughing die.
I watch the sunlight kiss the stream,
  And watch the stream curve in and out,
And here while at my work I dream,
  I struggle with the cunning trout.

The same old stream of long ago!
  I know its every turn and nook,
And all the flowering plants that grow,
  Nodding their blossoms at the brook.
And here I bend upon my knee,
  To let my fish line float ahead,
And by the hook, a trout I see,
  Listening to hear my tread.

The same old dam beside the mill;
  The same old bridge and waterfall;
The old-time music of the rill,
  And the old-time joy in all.
The birds that fluttered everywhere,
  The humble trees that bowed so low,
The living pleasure in the air
  All as of long ago.

71

Yet in the busy haunts of men,
  And wilderness of city streets,
I labor as I see again
  The days of perished joys and sweets.
The fishing rod, the speckled trout,
  The rippling water of the stream,
The gay birds fluttering about—
  I see, but in a dream.

And as I toil, and tire, and dream
  Of those old scenes—ofttimes my thoughts
Brighten and catch the heavenly gleam
  Of those dear old forget-me-nots.
Perchance I sing good Izaak's song—
  " I in these flowery meads would be,"
For laboring faithfully and long,
  " These crystal streams should solace me."

DO THE DEAD LEAVE US?

Do the dead leave us or do we leave them?
The world is a strange one when they are gone,
And the ways we travel on alone
Are not the bright ways we have known.
For the night is dark and there is no dawn,
When the hand of our loved one is first withdrawn;
And all we can say, as our tears we shed,
Are the voiceless words—"Our friend is dead."

Do the dead leave us or do we leave them?
When they are departing, we seem to take
A step that is one of fearful change,
And the world we are in grows cold and strange.
Our thoughts as our passage-way we make,
Are the thoughts of those but half awake.
Yet we try to explain our pain and dread
With the voiceless words—"Our friend is dead."

Do the dead leave us or do we leave them?
It is easily asked—but none respond—
So we lay them away in the grave below,
But what death is, none of us know,
Or what awaits the heart beyond,
That it loses those it held so fond.
Well may we touch the pall's pure hem,
Asking—"Do they leave us or do we leave them?"

SING ON.

Sing of the spring when the winter comes,
  Sing of the pleasures gone;
Sing a song of the bright glad hours,
  When the hours of darkness dawn.
When the autumn leaves fall on the lawn,
And the cold, wet days are coming on,
Then sing of the hours of spring;
Then sing of the hours of spring.

Sing of youth when old age draws near.
  Sing of the new-born rose;
Sing of the day that has just come in,—
  Life's morn and not life's close.
When the autumn leaves fall on the lawn,
And the cold, wet days are coming on,
Then sing of the hours of spring;
Then sing of the hours of spring.

THE SECRET MAN.

If you knew me within my world of thought—
  My world of thought where I alone am king,
Would that realm be a fragrant garden spot,
A place of bloom not easily forgot—
  A place where birds would pause entranced to sing?

Look on my deeds: I listen while you chide.
  Misjudge me if you will—you know me not;
If I am lacking, still I am untried,
But tell me would I gaze thus evil-eyed,
  From out the secret realm of thought?

Sometimes I wish that that same realm of mine
  Might be our meeting place; that we might there
Confer together where my fancies twine
Themselves into a kind of living vine—
  Confer together with our minds laid bare.

It might not be your fortune there to find
  The one whose deeds the world points boldly out,
But you could seek his face, with eyes less blind,
And find his manner—ah, perhaps more kind!
  And yet that manner all the world may doubt.

May doubt, I say, and see but selfish aim;
  May doubt and make a hero but a fraud,
Debase a kingdom or extol a name
As empty as the shallowness of fame.
  Could we but know as we are known of God!

Aye! were we known but in our worlds of thought—
  Our worlds of thought where each himself is king,
Would each be found a fragrant garden spot,
A place of bloom not easily forgot—
  A place where birds would pause entranced to sing?

GOIN' TO THE POORHOUSE.

Some folks from over the poorhouse
  Are comin' here today,
And I suppose as much as we hate to
  We've got to be took away.
My heart has long been dreadin'
  And my eyes I can't keep dry—
But I jes' came over, Nancy,
  To tell your folks, "Goodbye."

We've allus been good neighbors,
  And I hate to part like this;
But we can't have it made no different—
  Yet I know how I shall miss.
The home and the scenes and loved ones,
  And even the patch of sky
That smiles down over the meadow—
  But I came jes' to say "Goodbye."

Yes, I know in my dreams at the poorhouse
  I shall see all these scenes so dear,
And wake to find that I'm weepin'
  For you and the rest left here.
I say to myself it's folly,
  And try to keep back the sigh:
But I jes' came over, Nancy,
  To tell your folks, "Goodbye."

Well, Nancy, you'll not forget us—
　　Us two old folks you know.
We'll remember you for brightenin'
　　Our lives since long ago.
We may never meet again, dear,
　　Until we meet on high;
But I jes' came over, Nancy,
　　To tell your folks, "Goodbye."

Well, goodbye, Jim and Sarah—
　　But wait, before I go;
Here, Jim, is a knife John sent you—
　　'Tis little we have, you know.
And for each of you girls a ribbon
　　I bought: 'tis little, but One on high
Knows that great love goes with them—
　　But I came jes' to say " Goodbye."

Now, goodbye all; be careful
　　And good to yourselves, and pray
That we who are separated
　　May meet on some brighter day.
There, don't take on a weepin',
　　Jes' keep those dear eyes dry;
But they're waitin' for me at the corner
　　And so I must say "Goodbye."

A LOVE SONG.

How little can the sorrowing heart interpret
  The music of the heart that sings in mirth:
How undervalued is the transient beauty
  Of the stars, as viewed by humans from the earth.
The rose but little dreams of the affection
  Half hidden in the cooing of the doves—
The world is full of pure love undiscovered—
  There's never any heart but what it loves.

The flowers breathe their fragrance on the meadows,
  The sunshine throws its light upon the lawn;
There is love in every shadow of the night time—
  There is love in every ray of light at dawn.
The human heart is watered by the sunshine,
  And it loves when sunshine fades away for grief:
Love is sweeter than the flowers which we worship,
  And it only asks for trusting and belief.

The birds are ever flooding woods with music,
  But the woods their love have little guessed;
There is human love that finds no understanding,
  Although that love hath ofttimes been expressed.
The way the wind made love seemed harsh and cruel
  To the frail, pale flowers which it fanned:
My words and actions, too, seem rude and heartless—
  I love you, sweetheart, can't you understand?

JIM'S DEAD.

Jim's dead. Of all us children Jim
Was youngest, and we looked on him
As sorter in our way, fer he
Wuz deaf and dumb—of course you see
We loved him, but he'd only smile
In deepest silence all the while.
And so it sorter spoiled our play
To speak the words he couldn't say—
And know while lookin' in our eyes
He couldn't hear our words and cries.

Jim's dead—and when us children heard
That he wuz dead—there wa'n't a word
Of pity that we said fer him,
We all were silent jes' like Jim.
And I, who thought I felt the worst,
And chokin' like my heart would burst,
Went out into the orchard, there
To sorter drown away despair—
And there, a-lyin' on the ground,
Quite unaware I wuz around,
Jack sobbed and kept a-cryin' "Jim"—
And I—I didn't trouble him.

And then I found the old hay-mow:
I found it—I don't know jes' how,
Fer eyes don't count, to me it 'pears
When sorrow fills 'em up with tears.

Then when I thought myself alone
I heard a choked and stifled moan,
And Bill lay at my feet and clutched
His hair—and with his fingers touched
His eyes, as if to feel about,
To see if he had wept 'em out.

Jim didn't seem to count—and yet,
His silent way we can't forget.
And somehow when we saw him there,
His face as life-like and as fair
As ever; and his form so weak;
His lips that seemed to try to speak—
Somehow we children couldn't say
The words we might of yesterday,
But all together sobbed and said,
" I wish that I had died instead;"
Then choked and turned to look at him—
Then looked away and murmured—"Jim."

NEW YEARS.

Darkness fades from the Eastern skies,
And the world awakes at the new sunrise.
The pall of sorrow, pain and fear
Clings to the form of the old dead year,
And hope, with its heavy bands withdrawn
Rises again at the New Year's dawn.

HEROES OF OURS.

A tribute to those who manned the unfortunate battleship Maine which was wrecked in Havana harbor on the night of February 15th, 1898, and to those who were bereaved through the terrible incident.

Be it upon the battlefield, strewn with its ranks of dead,
The soldier breathes his last, 'tis there some tears for him
      are shed ;
Or if on weary beds of pain his final glances rest,
E'en there some loving nurse shall cross his hands upon his
      breast.
Be it upon some foreign shore they lay his form away,
Some tears will even there be his and prayers be said that
      day—
Some pity shall be his that day, some prayers shall reach
      the skies—
A soldier's death is always mourned, where'er a soldier dies.

Heroes of ours, who died for us, our hearts go out to you
In everlasting love for hearts that never beat untrue:
Though you must sleep 'neath other sod, where other
      banners wave,
The whole wide land you loved shall be for you a cherished
      grave.
Our tears shall fall throughout that grave as tender as the
      dew,
And we will bow above the spot and murmur love for you,
And it shall be forever green with fairest buds and flowers,
While still with pride we'll speak of thee and call thee ever
      ours.

Your dreams had often been to raise your country's colors
    high
Above the din of battle, and amid the smoke to die.
To you all other kind of death seemed only waste of life,
While glory rested on the eye that closed on scenes of strife.
Not so! a hero's life can find no low ignoble end,
Whatever strickening form of death the vaulted Heavens
    send;
His heroism leaves him not, until departs his breath—
No matter how a soldier dies, he meets a soldier's death.

And may the sweetest sleep be yours, and fairest blossoms
    grace
The very quietude that fills your silent resting place,
And if the Dead can feel or know the love of anything,
We pray, your ears at morn may hear the robin pause to sing.
But should the storm beat harsh—we ask the God that
    rules above,
For love of us to shield the place where lie the ones we love;
And He will hear our earnest prayers and guard thee safe-
    ly—thus,
For we would die if need there were for those who died for us.

      *   *   *   *   *   *

And we would pay our debt to you, sad homes left desolate,
And mourn for you made cheerless now by that stern hand
    of Fate.
Your sorrow is a common one, your tears fall not alone,
Our hearts respond in sobbing like the throbbing of your own.
Oh! Time be kind and spare them from the pain too great
    to bear,
Oh! make their ways still pleasant though their loved ones
    walk not there;
Forbid their hearts to languish for the faces that they miss—
The husband's word at parting or the lost boy's farewell kiss.

Though bereavement hovers o'er you like the darkness of
    the night,
It will fade as do the shadows at the mornings's dawning
    light;
Though the sunshine seems to vanish in the sad and silent
    pall,
There is still some hope to whisper—" Earth's existence is
    not all."
You must listen for the summons that shall call you from
    the fray—
It may come to you tomorrow, it may come to you today;
Those you love are calling for you and some day you must
    respond,
Earth's poor homes are not so distant from the better homes
    beyond.

And the wounded and the dying, we would ask our God to
    spare.
If it be Thy will, O Father, hear and grant this heartfelt
    prayer;
May a peace and comfort cheer them in their suffering and
    pain
May they live to bless their loved ones with their presence
    once again.
Well we know, our praise is silent in the presence of the
    tomb,
And our words grow cold and feeble in the shadow and the
    gloom;

As we pay an earnest tribute to the life-blood bravely shed,
We would give it to the living as we pay it to the Dead.

    *   *   *   *   *   *

And some there are, above whose graves no weeping friends
    may meet;

The sea birds are their mourners and the waves their wind-
      ing sheet,
But our hearts reach o'er the water and a careful watch
      they keep
Of the memory of the perished in the caverns of the deep.
Our tears may fall not on the spot nor there the robin sing,
And yet we would not idly stand and make no offering:
Our words go out in praise to them—to their poor senseless
      clay,
Our tears shall consecrate to them their Decoration Day.

And in the city of the Dead, wherever dead may be,
Heroes of ours, immortal shrines of love shall stand to thee.
We hold it true—our Dead is ours—and is no lasting loss—
Else o'er our graves no more should fall the shadow of the
      cross.
The dead shall lie in even ranks that Death shall level not,
And we shall find within those ranks the ones we each have
      sought;
And one thought lieth near our hearts, taught by believing
      thus—
The Dead we love though dead they are, are never dead to us.

Be it upon the battlefield, strewn with its ranks of dead,
The soldier breathes his last, 'tis there some tears for him
      are shed.
Or if on weary beds of pain his final glances rest
E'en there some loving nurse shall cross his hands upon his
      breast.
Be it upon some foreign shore they lay his form away,
Some tears will even there be his and prayers be said that
      day—
Some pity shall be his that day, some prayers shall reach
      the skies—
A soldier's death is always mourned, where'er a soldier dies.

www.ingramcontent.com/pod-product-compliance
Lightning Source LLC
Chambersburg PA
CBHW032158010726
47493CB00008BA/2741